# Nobby T
# to Fra(

by Darren & Julia Spence

This book belongs to:

"Night night, Nobby!"

The Chocolate Labrador puppy settled down in his basket. His owner switched off the kitchen lights and shut the door. He heard the stairs creaking, and then it was quiet.

He should be going to sleep now. But something told Nobby it was not a night for sleep. He sniffed the air. Amongst the wafts of tonight's dinner and damp boots drying by the fire, there was something else – a whiff of magic.

It was a clear night, and the moon shone brightly through the kitchen window. Nobby looked across at the back door and the moonbeam falling on the dog flap.

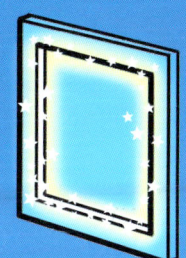

He got out of his basket by the fire and crept across the shiny kitchen floor towards the door. He paused, wagged his tail with excitement then leapt through his dog flap.

Nobby yelped as he landed on a hard pavement. When he had turned himself the right way up, he found himself standing right next to another dog.

Nobby had never seen a dog quite like this before. She had beautiful soft apricot-coloured fur which grew in little pompoms on her head, tail and legs. Underneath her long, curling eyelashes, her dark eyes rested on Nobby, and he felt himself go slightly pink under his chocolate-brown fur.

"Bonjour," she said, in a soft voice.

"Er …" said Nobby.

"Ah! you are English, non?"

"Non … er – yes, er …" said Nobby, fumbling for words. "I'm Nobby, and I'm, I'm …"

"It's nice to meet you, Nobby. My name is Trixabelle. Perhaps you 'ave not seen French poodle before, non? Perhaps you 'ave not been to Paris before?"

"No, I haven't, but I'm very pleased to meet you," said Nobby, bowing slightly.

Trixabelle nodded her head in return, then looked up and said, "Nobby! Do not move!"

Trixabelle's command sounded so urgent that Nobby looked around in alarm.

"Non! Stay as you are!" said Trixabelle.

Nobby did as he was told. Then, for the first time since his arrival, he began to notice his surroundings. He was in a busy square that seemed to be full of little stalls. Each stall was hung with lots of pictures, and some of the stallholders were drawing or painting.

Then he realised that there was a man drawing very close to where he was standing. The man kept looking over the top of his board and staring very intently at Nobby.

"You like 'aving your portrait done?" said Trixabelle, smiling. "Don't worry, Nobby. Zis artist is my owner. Sometimes when 'e 'as no customers who want zer portrait done, zen 'e draws me. And now, 'e is drawing you, too!"

Nobby's body was beginning to ache from keeping so still, and he was very relieved when the artist had finished. He turned the picture round to show it to Nobby.

"C'est bon?"

Before Nobby had a chance to see, a young couple strolled up and started talking to the artist. The woman was wearing a yellow coat, a red scarf and a strong perfume that tickled Nobby's nose. She was pointing to the picture.

Trixabelle's fluffy ears were pinned back.

"Zey really like ze picture," she explained to Nobby. "Zey say it looks just like zer own dog, and zey want to buy it!"

And sure enough, after a few minutes, the couple were walking away with the picture, which had been carefully rolled and tied with a red ribbon.

Nobby was disappointed not to get a good look at the picture, and now he would never see it again. His nose drooped towards the pavement. Suddenly, his eye was caught by something red. It was the woman's scarf. She must have dropped it.

Nobby knew immediately that he must give it back to her and without a further thought, he picked the scarf up in his mouth and set off.

"Nobby, non! Zis way!" Trixabelle barked. She had spotted the young couple on the other side of the road, heading towards one of the cafés.

The edge of the square was filled with cafés, all of them spilling onto the pavement. At nearly every table there were people eating and drinking and enjoying the spring sunshine.

Nobby and Trixabelle wandered around, looking for the young couple with the picture. But there were so many people.

They spent several minutes weaving through chairs and legs, but there was no sign of the woman with the yellow coat. They sat down by one of the tables for a rest.

Almost immediately, one of the waiters appeared with two bowls of water and some curious-looking buns.

"Croissants," explained Trixabelle. "Zey are like a sort of bread. 'Ere in France, people eat zem for breakfast."

Nobby quite liked the taste of the croissant, but by the time he'd finished, he seemed to have lots of it stuck to his fur. Somehow, Trixabelle had managed to eat hers without making such a mess.

"I am afraid we 'ave lost ze owner of ze scarf, Nobby," said Trixabelle. Nobby sighed heavily, and had to admit it was true.

"Come on," said Trixabelle, "I will show you ze best view in Paris. Zat will be fun, non?"

Trixabelle got up to lead the way, and Nobby wondered what he should do with the scarf. He decided to take it with him, just in case.

Nobby followed Trixabelle down the road to a bus stop where some people were waiting. When the bus came, the two dogs slipped unnoticed into the crowd and got on.

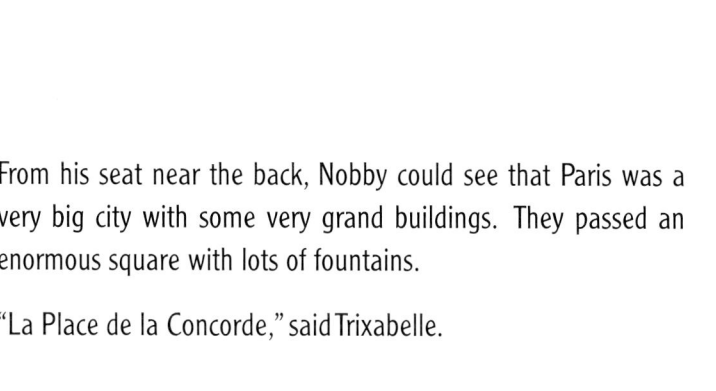

From his seat near the back, Nobby could see that Paris was a very big city with some very grand buildings. They passed an enormous square with lots of fountains.

"La Place de la Concorde," said Trixabelle.

Before long, Trixabelle said they had reached their stop, and they made their way off the bus.

It was an amazing view. They were now by a big river, and looming over the water was the most enormous tower that just went up and up and up.

"And zis … is ze Eiffel Tower!" Trixabelle announced.

"Yes, it is a wonderful view," agreed Nobby, putting the scarf down for a moment.

"Non!" cried Trixabelle, "zat is not ze view! We will get ze view when we are up ze tower."

"You mean, we are going up it?" said Nobby.

"Mais, oui – but, of course!" said Trixabelle.

Trixabelle led the way, and they slipped into a group of people going through an entrance at the bottom of the tower. They began to climb some steps.

They climbed ...

... and they climbed ...

... and they climbed ...

... and they climbed.

Nobby's legs began to feel quite tired, but Trixabelle was showing no signs of slowing down.

"There are a lot of steps," he mumbled through the scarf. "Yes," said Trixabelle, "one thousand, six 'undred and sixty-five to ze top."

Nobby dropped the scarf and looked at Trixabelle. "One thousand six hundred and sixty-five!" he repeated, in disbelief.

"Zat's right," said Trixabelle. She gave a cheeky grin, then said, "But do not worry. We're not going to ze top, only to ze second floor."

Just when Nobby thought his legs would not take him up another step, they arrived. He carefully put the scarf down so he could get his breath back and take in the view.

The city of Paris spread out in every direction as far as the eye could see. There were tree-lined avenues, enormous squares and graceful arches.

"C'est magnifique!" breathed Trixabelle.

"Yes – that is, oui – it's magnificent!" Nobby agreed.

He picked up the scarf again, and he and Trixabelle wandered around the second floor platform. There were lots of people, all admiring the view and taking photographs.

Suddenly, Nobby sneezed. Something was tickling his nose; something scented. Then he saw what it was. The young woman with the yellow coat was standing just a few steps away.

Nobby trotted over to her, his tail wagging with excitement.

The woman recognised Nobby immediately.

"Le petit chien!" she exclaimed.

Then she saw what Nobby was carrying in his mouth, and said, "Ah, tu es très gentil."

"She says you are very kind," said Trixabelle, coming up beside him.

The young couple both made an enormous fuss of Nobby. They told him what a clever dog he was and how grateful they were. Then the young woman noticed that Nobby's eyes were fixed on the rolled up picture, and it seemed as if she understood. She picked it up, took off the red ribbon, and unrolled the picture so that Nobby and Trixabelle could see.

"C'est magnifique!" said Trixabelle. Nobby thought so, too.

Whilst the woman was wrapping her picture up again, Trixabelle whispered to Nobby that it was time to go.

"We can go down in ze lift," she said.

"There's a lift?" said Nobby. "You mean, we needn't have climbed all those stairs?"

Trixabelle gave Nobby a cheeky look. "But it was such fun!" she said.

It was much quicker going down in the lift. At the bottom, the doors opened and Nobby jumped out, eager to find out where Trixabelle was going to take him next. He looked round to see where she was, but the doors were closing behind him.

"Au revoir, Nobby!" he heard her soft voice calling. Then the doors clanged shut.

Trixabelle was gone, so had the Paris pavements and the spring sunshine.

Nobby found himself in a dark place with a smooth floor and a familiar smell. He was in his own cosy kitchen.

Feeling very sleepy, he padded over to his basket by the fire, flopped onto the blanket and fell fast asleep.

"Morning Nobby!"

Nobby stirred as his owner came into the kitchen and pulled back the curtains.

"I don't know why you're always so sleepy in the mornings! And what's all this?"

She bent over and started brushing something off his coat.

Nobby opened a bleary eye to see the last few bits of croissant flying onto the floor.

"It looks like you're covered in bits of … what is it, pastry?"

Nobby licked a crumb from his paw and wagged his tail. His owner patted him fondly, then stopped and wrinkled her nose.

"And why do you smell of perfume? Honestly, Nobby, anyone would think you'd got a girlfriend!"

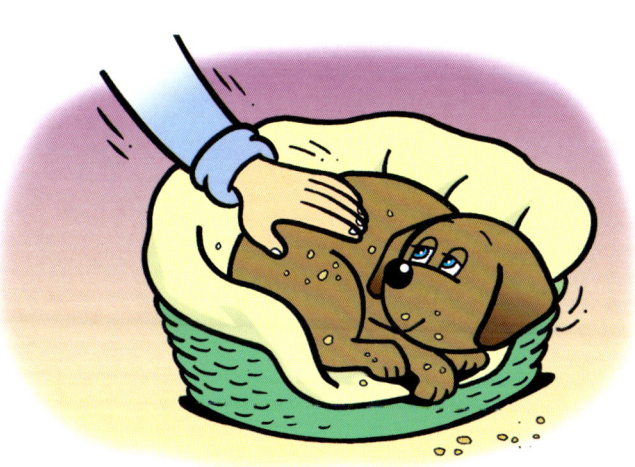

NORBY TRAVELS TO FRANCE

Facts about **France** ...

| | |
|---|---|
| Capital City: | **Paris** |
| Money: | **€ Euro** |
| French Dog: | **Poodle** |
| A Famous Landmark: | **The Eiffel Tower** |
| Language Spoken: | **French** |
| Flying Time from London, England: | **45 Minutes** |

NOBBY TRAVELS TO FRANCE

# Become a Nobby Traveller !

If you enjoyed this "Nobby Travels" story, why not join our exclusive members club and become a Nobby Traveller? When you join, you'll receive:

- ★ a Nobby Traveller passport to record your travels
- ★ a Nobby Traveller bag
- ★ a set of Nobby Travels stickers
- ★ Money-off vouchers

... **plus**, you'll have access to the members-only area of the Nobby Travels website, where you can:

- ★ download loads of cool stuff
- ★ take part in competitions
- ★ keep up to date with news about Nobby

To become a Nobby Traveller, simply visit www.nobbytravels.com/nobbytraveller

**All for just £5 per year**

BOBBY TRAVELS TO FRANCE